The Great Minu

The Great Minu

BETH P. WILSON

Illustrated by Jerry Pinkney

Based on "The Honourable Minu," originally published in
West African Folk Tales by George Harrap & Company Ltd.,
London, England

Follett Publishing Company / Chicago

To Ghanya, with love

Introduction

Since ancient times storytelling has been important
throughout the great continent of Africa. Long ago, people in
villages would gather together in the evenings and tell
stories. Often they would sit in a circle around an open fire.
Sometimes one person would begin a story only to have
others continue it until the story's end. The tales were both
entertaining and clever, often with animals playing tricks on
other animals or on people. Usually the wrongdoer was
punished in some way.

Some storytellers journeyed from village to village, weaving
a magic spell with tales of the tricky hare or the clever
spider, and learning new stories as they moved along. Often
the listeners would clap their hands, beat on drums, or dance
during or after the storytelling.

Today African children are just as excited about telling and
listening to folktales as were their parents and grandparents
before them. In West African villages, families often gather
in the early evening after a meal of foo-foo (cooked yam balls
dipped in vegetable-beef stew). Soon someone in the group,
usually a grandmother, begins a story. Frequently the story
is "The Great Minu," which has long been a favorite of
young and old.

Across the ocean and far away, a poor African
farmer prepared to make a journey to the big city of
Accra. He walked around his small farm, taking
note of the yams and corn growing in the garden.
Then he fed his chickens and goats, latched his
thatched-roof hut, and took off down the narrow,
dusty road.

7

8   The farmer hummed happily to himself as the morning sun came into view. How exciting to be going to the big city! Nothing much happened in his tiny village, but since Accra was the largest city in Ghana, he would find much excitement there.

After walking for some time, he stopped to rest under a tulip tree. He leaned against the tree trunk and breathed in the morning air. Birds swooped and soared in the sunshine, but no man, woman, or child traveled the dusty road in either direction.

Soon he jumped to his feet and started down the
road again. As he reached the first village along the
way, he saw a woman on her knees, washing clothes
in a stream of water. "Good day!" he called to the
woman. "I'm on my way to the big city—I'm on my
way to Accra!" The woman just smiled and went
on washing her clothes.

12 Farther down the road he saw some men and boys making iron. They were too busy to look up when he passed, but he called out just the same. "Good day! I'm on my way to the big city—I'm on my way to Accra!" The men and boys stopped for a moment and nodded. Then they went on working as if he hadn't spoken.

Soon he saw a grandmother telling stories to her
little grandchildren. The traveler loved a story and
was tempted to stop. But he knew he must be on
his way. He waved his hand high and called out,
"Good day! I'm on my way to the big city—I'm on
my way to Accra!" The children turned to look, and
the grandmother smiled and waved. Then she went
on telling her story.

16   The traveler trudged along until he felt tired and hungry. Finding a cool spot, he sat down by the side of the road and opened his lunch bag. He ate a piece of chicken and a big red banana. Then he took a short nap under a cocoa tree.

As soon as the traveler woke up, he started off again because he still had quite a long way to go.

At last he approached some farms on the outskirts of Accra. The first thing he noticed was a great herd of cows. He wondered who could own such a herd. Seeing a man with them, he asked, "To whom do these cows belong?"

The man did not know the language of the traveler, so he shrugged his shoulders and said, "Minu," meaning, "I do not understand."

The traveler thought Minu must be a person, and so he exclaimed, "Mr. Minu must be very rich!"

Entering the city, the traveler saw some large new buildings in the town square. He wondered who might own the fine buildings. But the man he asked could not understand his question, so he answered, "Minu."

"Good heavens!" cried the traveler. "What a rich fellow Mr. Minu must be to own all those cows and all these buildings, too!"

Soon he came to a great hotel surrounded by beautiful grounds and mahogany trees. A group of fashionably dressed African ladies came down the front steps of the hotel. The traveler stepped up to them and asked who might be the owner of such a grand hotel.

The ladies smiled and said softly, "Minu."

"How wealthy Mr. Minu is!" exclaimed the astonished traveler.

24 He wandered from one neighborhood to another. Seeing a large house with many columns and porches, he stopped in surprise. "These homes in Accra are so grand—not a bit like the huts of my village," he said. Just then a servant came out. The traveler stepped up hurriedly and asked, "Please tell me who owns this fine house."

The young woman humped her shoulders. "Minu," she mumbled.

"How foolish of me to ask," the traveler said. "The Great Minu, of course." He stood for a moment, admiring the house and garden. Then he went on.

Finally he came to the harbor, where he saw men
loading bananas, cocoa beans, and mahogany onto
a huge ship. The blue sky above, the foamy green
ocean below, and the sailors rushing about on board
ship made quite a sight. Surprised at the great
cargo, the traveler inquired of a bystander, "To
whom does this fine vessel belong?"

"Minu," replied the puzzled man who couldn't
understand a word the traveler said.

"To the Great Minu also?" the traveler asked. "He
is the richest man I ever heard of!"

Just as the traveler was setting out for home, he saw
men carrying a coffin down the main street of
Accra. A long procession, all dressed in black,
followed the men. People on the sidelines shook
their heads slowly. Sad faces looked up now and
then. When the traveler asked one of the mourners
the name of the dead person, he received the usual
reply, "Minu."

29

"Mr. Minu is dead?" wailed the traveler. "Poor Mr. Minu! So he had to leave all his wealth—his herd of cows, his buildings, his grand hotel, and his fine ship —and die just like a poor person. Well, well, in the future I'll be content to live a simple life, to breathe the fresh air on my little farm, and to help the poor people in my little village."

The long dusty road back didn't seem as long as it had before. When the farmer arrived home, he unlatched the door of his hut and looked around inside. Then he climbed into his own snug bed and dreamed of the good foo-foo he would eat the next day.